Minji's Salon

By Eun-hee Choung

Kane/Miller
BOOK PUBLISHERS

For my niece, Yeon Woo

Kane/Miller Book Publishers, Inc.
First American Edition 2008
by Kane/Miller Book Publishers, Inc.
La Jolla, California

First published in South Korea in 2007 by Sang Publishing.
Text and illustrations copyright © Choung, Eun-hee 2007

For information contact:
Kane/Miller Book Publishers, Inc.
P.O. Box 8515
La Jolla, CA 92038
www.kanemiller.com

Library of Congress Control Number: 2007932511
Printed and bound in China
1 2 3 4 5 6 7 8 9 10

ISBN: 978-1-933605-67-8

Minji's Salon

By Eun-hee Choung

Good morning, madam.
What would you like today?

Perhaps something like this?

Choosing the right style can be difficult.
(Wigs, for example, don't suit everyone.)

The color must be mixed carefully.
(No tasting allowed.)

You have to be patient; beauty takes time.

A little more color…

And then, you have to wait…a little longer…keep still!

We're almost done…

Just the finishing touches…

What do you think?

Mom will be back soon. I think she'll be surprised.

She is!

"My goodness!
Are you the owner of this salon?"

"Yes madam.
Would you like to make an appointment?"